Belle's Journey

WRITTEN BY MARILYNN REYNOLDS
ILLUSTRATED BY STEPHEN McCALLUM

EVERY Saturday on the great wide prairie, Molly rode her brown mare Belle to piano lessons. Eight miles to the piano teacher's house and eight miles home.

On hot summer days they rode under a high yellow sun and a blue sky. In winter they trudged along the trails beneath grey skies and a low pale sun that gave no warmth.

Molly rode bareback, as there was no money for a saddle. Sometimes in winter when the trails were rough, she would slip and tumble off the horse's back into the snow. When that happened, Belle always stopped and turned her long, kind face around to see if Molly was all right. Then the mare would wait patiently while the little girl scrambled up onto her back again before she resumed her slow, measured gait along the trail.

Belle was an old horse. Her back was bony and her mane was thin. She couldn't prance and gallop the way she had when she was young.

"Belle's showing her age," Molly's father said one day. "She's getting slow and she's not strong enough to pull the plough or the big wagons anymore. I think maybe we should sell her and buy you a new pony."

At first Molly was excited. I'll race into town on my new pony, she thought. I'll tie ribbons in her mane; I'll braid her tail and enter her in the fair. She'll win first prize for sure.

But then Molly wondered who would buy Belle. What other child would ride her to school? What other child would comb her? Who would bring her special things to eat?

One cold winter day, Molly rode into town for her piano
lesson. Belle waited patiently outside while Molly played her
scales and pieces for the teacher. After the lesson Belle slowly set
out on the long journey home. Molly carried her music books in
her shiny new leather satchel and wore a heavy jacket and wool
pants to keep out the snow and the cold.

At first the winter sky was clear and the snow sparkled in a thousand colours like crushed glass. But halfway home, a few hard, cold flakes of snow drifted across their path. Molly looked up. The sky had darkened to an angry grey.

Molly dug her heels into the horse's sides. "Come on Belle," she said, urging the old horse into a trot.

Soon it was snowing steadily. An icy wind began to howl as it blew the snow over the land. There was no escaping the storm now. Within minutes the wind was hurling sheets of snow across the fields. Molly and Belle were caught in a blizzard.

Molly was afraid of blizzards. On the prairie there were few trees. Terrible fires had burned the woods off the land long ago. Now there were no barriers left to stop the blowing snow. Sometimes blizzards raged for days and days, piling the snow in great drifts right over the farmhouses. The families inside couldn't open their doors and were imprisoned in their homes until they could dig their way out. Every winter a few people would become lost in their own yard and freeze to death. So in the fall, Molly's father tied a long rope from the door of the farmhouse all the way to the handle on the barn door. If a blizzard blew in, he could follow the rope to the barn to feed the animals, then find his way back again through the blinding snow.

Molly was terrified. "It's a blizzard," she shouted above the storm. "Home, Belle!" The little girl's face was so cold, she could hardly move her mouth to call out. The snow flew into her eyes and cheeks, stinging like needles. The shriek of the wind filled her ears.

The horse broke into a canter along the frozen ground. Molly clung to Belle's mane, searching for a familiar building in the distance to guide them home. But it was useless. She could see nothing but snow swirling around them. Soon the trail was buried. Belle lowered her head and slowed to a deliberate plodding walk, and Molly could tell that the old horse was trying to feel the trail beneath the snow with her hooves, as only horses can.

Inside her heavy winter clothes, Molly's skin began to prickle and shiver. At first her toes burned as if they were on fire. But soon she couldn't even feel her toes or legs or cheeks or fingertips. She shut her eyes against the sting of the sharp snowflakes and held tighter to the horse's mane. Her music case slid away into the snow.

"Take me home, Belle," she prayed.

The old horse struggled on, head down. She turned and lunged into the drifts as she fought her way through the storm. All the world was a blur of white. Molly couldn't see anything around her. She couldn't tell the ground from the air. She didn't know if Belle was heading for home, or if every step was taking them farther and farther away.

Then suddenly for a few seconds the wind died and the snow stopped blowing. Belle came to a full stop. She lifted her head, pricked up her ears and gazed intently across the field. Molly opened her eyes and stared hard into the distance. Did Belle see something she recognized? At first Molly could see nothing but a thick, white blanket of snow. Then far away, she could just make out the vanes of a windmill. It was the windmill in her own farmyard.

As quickly as it had died, the wind picked up, and the windmill disappeared once more in the whirling snow. But Belle tossed her head and began to heave her way through the snow again. Molly's hands were too cold to hang onto the horse's mane any longer, so she flung her arms around Belle's neck and buried her face against the horse's snowy coat. She closed her eyes and hung on fiercely as the old horse laboured through the storm.

Much later, numb, stiff and halfway between sleeping and waking, Molly raised her head. Just in front of her, almost hidden in the storm, stood the familiar shape of their little farmhouse with its unpainted boards and its stovepipe pointing up to the sky. In the window a coal oil lamp shone dimly, and Molly thought she could see the silhouettes of her parents watching for her.

Belle had brought her home.

Molly's mother and father ran out of the house as the horse staggered to the door. Molly's clothes were frozen to Belle's back, and her father had to cut through them with a butcher's knife before he could lift his daughter down and carry her to the house.

Once the little girl was safely inside, her father ran out into the blizzard for the horse. Gripping the safety rope with one hand and her bridle with the other, he slowly led Belle through the storm into the barn.

The old horse stumbled on her stiff, cold legs as Molly's father threw open the door. Inside, the barn was warm from the body heat of the cows and pigs who shuffled quietly in the dark. Molly's father led Belle into her stall. He lit the lantern and turned to the old horse. Belle was coated with frost, and ice had formed around her mouth and nostrils. Ice covered each eye like a pane of glass.

Molly's father rubbed Belle down with a blanket and poured oats into her trough, but she was too tired to eat. Instead, the horse raised her head until her forehead met his. Father gently stroked her thin neck and mane as he felt the warmth slowly return to her long face and muzzle. Belle closed her eyes.

When Molly's father saw that the old horse was asleep, he gave her neck a last pat, blew out the light and headed out into the roar of the blizzard. He slid the barn door shut and groped his way along the rope like a blind man until he was back at the house where Molly and her mother were waiting.

Molly's father never talked about selling Belle again. The old horse continued to carry Molly to school and to piano lessons. She spent the warm summer days in the back pasture where the grass grew thickest and sweetest, and she slept with the other animals in the barn for the rest of her days.

To my mother, Jessie Boden Lloyd, who rode her pony eight miles to music lessons and who became one of Saskatchewan's early piano teachers.
M.C.R.

To June, my mother, and Jasmine for their faith and support.
S.M.

Text copyright © 1993 Marilynn Reynolds
Illustration copyright © 1993 Stephen McCallum

Publication assistance provided by The Canada Council.
First paperback printing, 1994

Orca Book Publishers
PO Box 5626 Stn. B
Victoria, B.C. Canada
V8R 6S4

Orca Book Publishers
#3028, 1574 Gulf Road
Point Roberts, WA USA
98281

Design by Christine Toller
Printed and bound in Hong Kong

Canadian Cataloguing in Publication Data
Reynolds, Marilynn, 1940–
Belle's journey

ISBN 1-55143-021-5

I. McCallum, Stephen, 1960–   II. Title.
PS8585.E96B4 1993   jC813'.54   C93-091076-1
PZ7.R49Be 1993